Let's Play Tag!

📖 Read the Page

▶ Read the Story

⭐ Game

😊 Yes ☹ No

🔁 Repeat

⬛ Stop

AIR PENGUIN

written by Scott Sonneborn
illustrated by Estudi Iboix

The penguins were flying the gang
back home to the zoo.

The trip had just
started when Skipper said,
"This is your Captain speaking.
The good news is we'll be landing
immediately. The bad news is
we're crash landing!"

3

The plane crashed in Africa.
"Good landing boys!" said Skipper.
"Who says penguins can't fly?"

The other animals looked worried.
They were far from their homes at
the zoo.

"You and your little friends just stay out of our hair," Skipper told Alex and Marty.

The penguins needed time to fix the plane. They also needed some spare parts.

The penguins waited for a truck full of tourists.

"Operation Tourist Trap is a go!" said Skipper.

Private flopped down in front of the truck. It screeched to a stop. The tourists got out and took pictures.

While the people were looking at Private, Rico started the engine.

Kowalski jumped into the truck and grabbed the steering wheel. The other penguins climbed in and they zoomed away!

Now the penguins had tools and spare parts to fix the plane. But they couldn't use them without thumbs.

Luckily, Phil and Mason both had some. And so did all the chimps they found!

"We've recruited a few extra thumbs for you, Skipper," announced Mason.

"Well, I'll be a monkey's uncle!" exclaimed Skipper.

"Oh, I doubt that," Mason said.

Skipper showed the chimpanzees his plans. They got right to work.

11

 But then the chimps stopped to take a banana break.

That wasn't part of the penguins' plan!

Skipper was angry. "You don't see penguins taking banana breaks!" he roared.

Skipper yelled, but the chimps didn't listen. They wanted their banana breaks. And they weren't going back to work until they got them.

The chimps went on strike!

Just then, Marty ran up.
Alex was in trouble!
Marty needed the plane
to save him.

Skipper turned to the
chimps. "If you take
banana breaks, the wings
will never be fixed in time
to save Alex!" he said.

"Actually," said Mason,
"the wings are fixed."

"Maybe so," said Skipper. "But if you chimps take breaks, it will take forever to fix the wheels."

"The wheels are fixed, too," said Mason.

"Okay," said Skipper. "But what about the hot chocolate machine?"

Mason just smiled and handed Skipper a cup of cocoa.

Skipper saw that chimpanzees may
not work like penguins, but they get
the job done.

"All right, you can have your banana
breaks," Skipper announced.

Ooo! Ooo! Ooo! The chimpanzees hooted for joy. They put down their signs, took a banana break, and then finished fixing the plane.

The plane roared into the air.

"Jump, chimps, jump,"
yelled Skipper.

A chain of chimps lowered a barrel to the ground. Alex hopped into the barrel. Working together, the penguins and the chimps saved Alex!

"When it comes to air travel,"
said Skipper, "we know you
have no choice whatsoever.
But thanks again for choosing Air Penguin!"

Penguin Pictures

confident

gloomy

confused

curious

MONKEYING AROUND

joyful

irritable

exhausted

startled

25

24,109 ×761469

Front View

$$u = \sqrt{\frac{2mg}{\rho A C_d}}$$

$$F(v_i \times v)^2 = SaRDINE$$

Power Loading . . . . . .
Power (Total) . . . . . .

Airfoil Se
Gross We
Root Chord
Dihedral

Power Loading 19.61
Power (Total) . . . . 840 w

Front View

F

$$(1/v/(2^{V-1})$$

168

Nose

Wing

13

24,109

PNGNS

Left
Right

61469

$$\frac{N^1}{N^2}$$

Wing Area . . . . 456 sq ft.
Root Chord . . . . 115 in
Dihedral . . . . 5° 3 f in
Aspect Ratio . . . 50

$$\left(\frac{CH_4 F_5 h}{H_2 O \rightleftharpoons O_2}\right) S^2 ar V$$

$$Ax = \lambda < RIE$$